FPL-PBK

D0360559

WELCOME TO
PASSPORT TO READING
A beginning reader's ticket to a brand-new world!

Every book in this program is designed to build read-along and read-alone skills, level by level, through engaging and enriching stories. As the reader turns each page, he or she will become more confident with new vocabulary, sight words, and comprehension.

These PASSPORT TO READING levels will help you choose the perfect book for every reader.

READING TOGETHER
Read short words in simple sentence structures together to begin a reader's journey.

READING OUT LOUD
Encourage developing readers to sound out words in more complex stories with simple vocabulary.

READING INDEPENDENTLY
Newly independent readers gain confidence reading more complex sentences with higher word counts.

READY TO READ MORE
Readers prepare for chapter books with fewer illustrations and longer paragraphs.

This book features sight words from the educator-supported Dolch Sight Words List. This encourages the reader to recognize commonly used vocabulary words, increasing reading speed and fluency.

For more information, please visit passporttoreadingbooks.com.

Enjoy the journey!

Cover design by Jamie Yee.

Little, Brown and Company
Hachette Book Group
1290 Avenue of the Americas, New York, NY 10104
Visit us at LBYR.com

First Edition: November 2017

Little, Brown and Company is a division of Hachette Book Group, Inc. The Little, Brown name and logo are trademarks of Hachette Book Group, Inc.

The publisher is not responsible for websites (or their content) that are not owned by the publisher.

Library of Congress Control Number 2017946360

ISBNs: 978-0-316-55784-9 (pbk.), 978-0-316-41622-1 (Scholastic edition), 978-0-316-55783-2 (ebook), 978-0-316-55785-6 (ebook), 978-0-316-55782-5 (ebook)

Printed in the United States of America

CW

10 9 8 7 6 5 4 3 2 1

Passport to Reading titles are leveled by independent reviewers applying the standards developed by Irene Fountas and Gay Su Pinnell in *Matching Books to Readers*: *Using Leveled Books in Guided Reading*, Heinemann, 1999.

NINJA PARTY!

Adapted by Jonathan Evans
Based on the episode "The Art of Ninjutsu"
written by Ben Gruber

LITTLE, BROWN AND COMPANY
New York   Boston

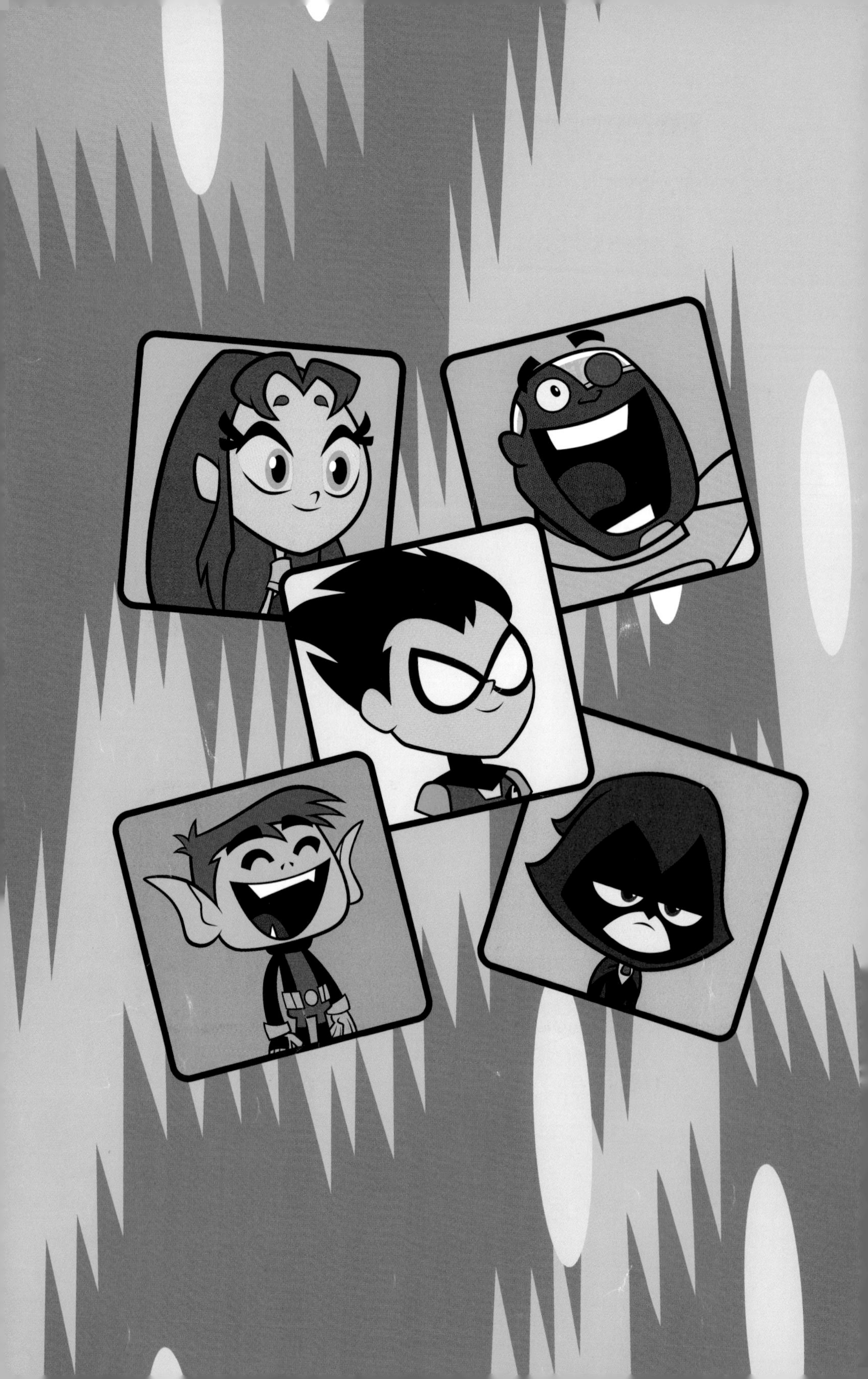

Attention, Teen Titans fans!
Look for these words when you read
this book. Can you spot them all?

pajamas

alarm

shuriken

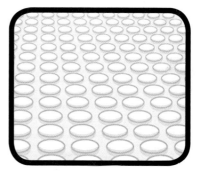

bubbles

The Teen Titans are on an important secret mission.

They must not be heard at all.
They must not be seen at all.

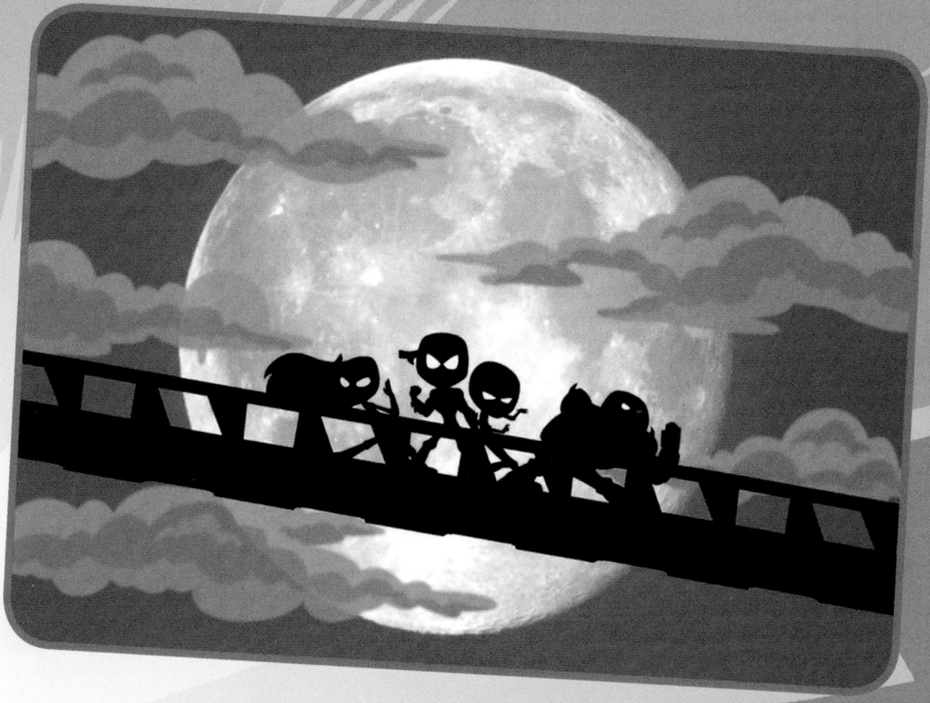

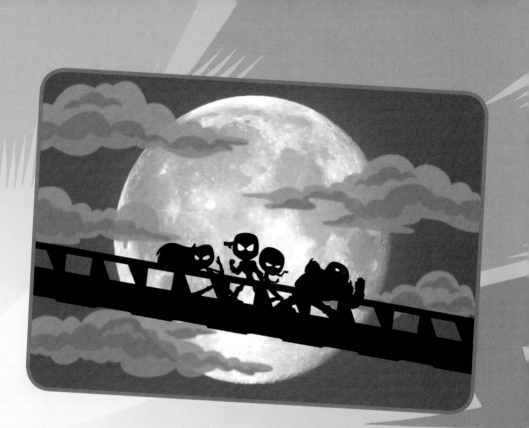

They must be...ninjas!

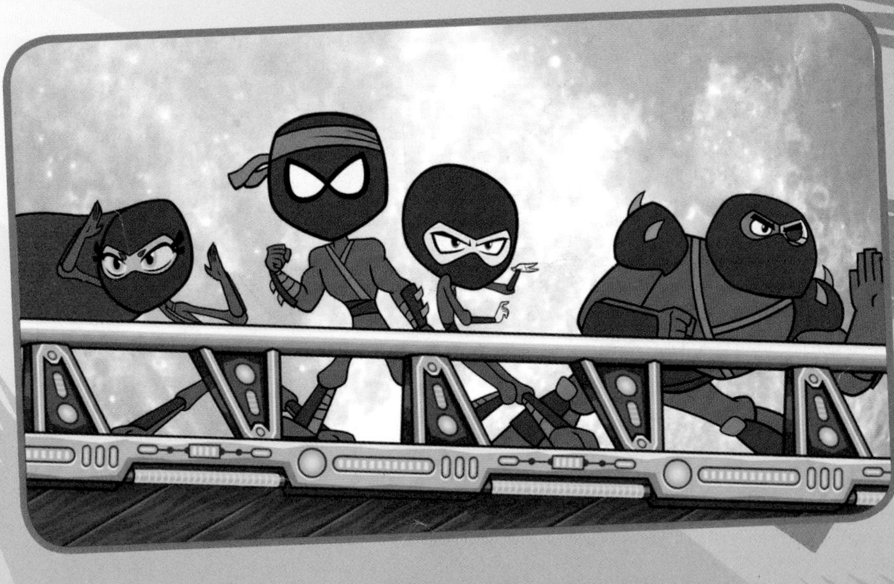

"Why are you all wearing pajamas?"
Beast Boy asks the other Titans.

"This is the garb of the ninja,"
Starfire says.
She kicks to prove her point.

"We cannot capture the MacGuffin without them," Robin explains seriously.

"What is a MacGuffin?" Beast Boy asks. He is confused.

"It is not important.
We must move...quietly,"
Robin says.

Just then, Beast Boy sees
something shiny.
"Oh, snap! A penny!" he yells.

His loud voice triggers a loud alarm.

"My bad," Beast Boy says.

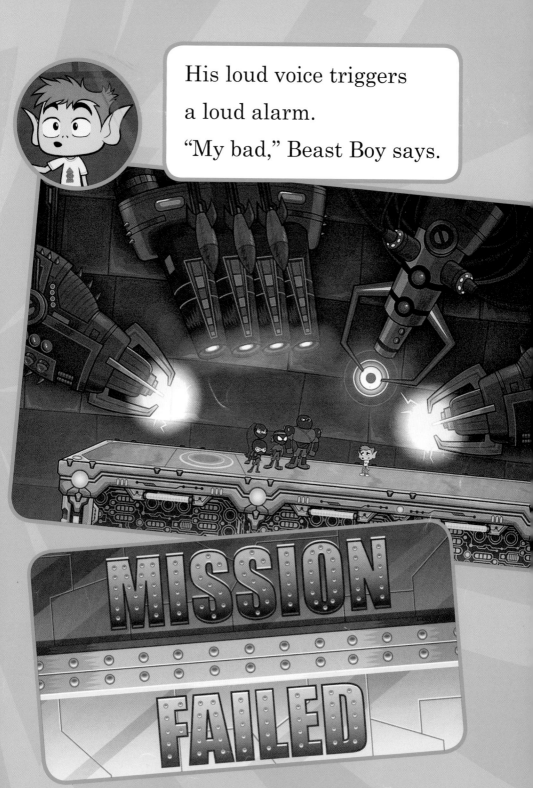

The Titans are mad at Beast Boy
for ruining their mission.

"Whatever.
Being a ninja is not fun,"
Beast Boy says.
His teammates are offended.

"Are you sure?" asks Cyborg, showing off his cool ninja moves.

Beast Boy is amazed.
"Whoa! Sick!" he exclaims.

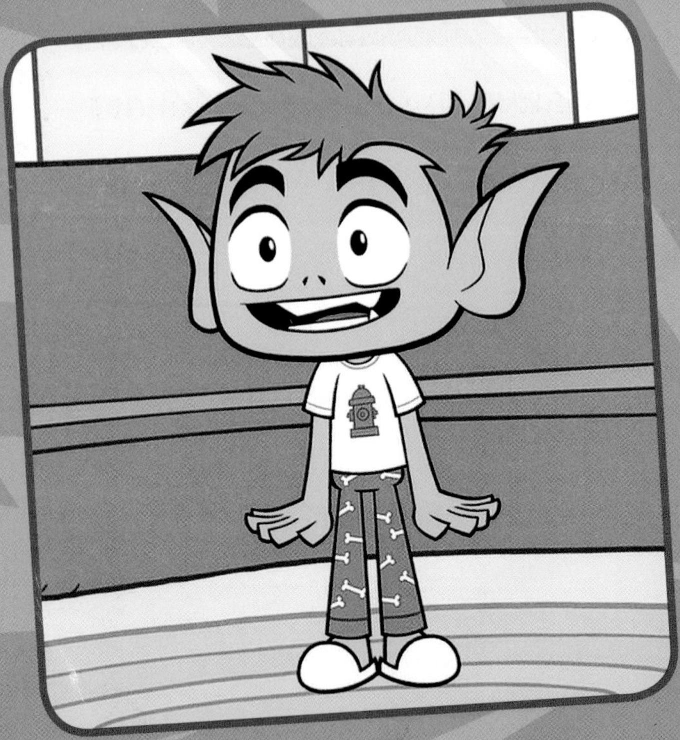

"NINJA!"
the Titans yell.

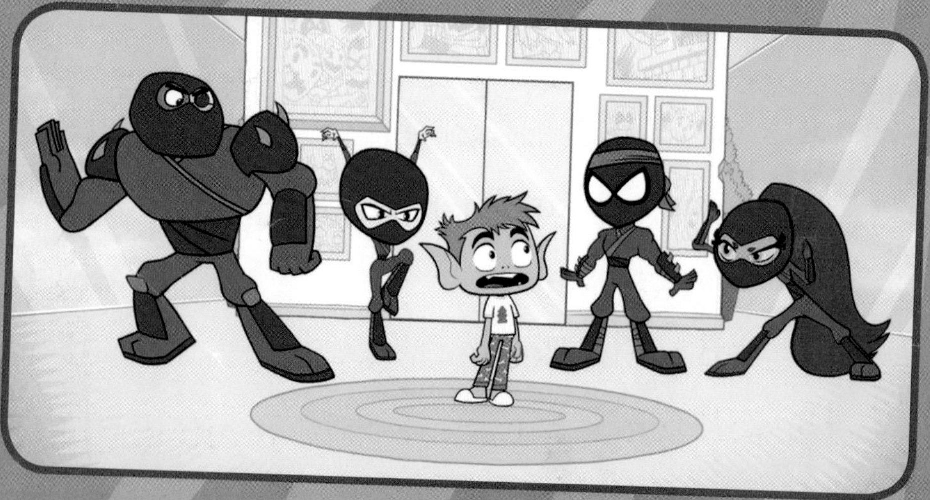

"You have to teach me the art of the ninja!" Beast Boy begs his friends.

Robin smiles under his mask.
"Very well," he says.
He will train Beast Boy.
He will teach him how to be a ninja.

LESSON ONE
DISGUISE

"A ninja must hide in plain sight," Robin says.

Beast Boy looks around.

The room is empty.

"Wait, where did he go?" he asks.

Robin jumps out
of hiding.
"Ninja!" he says.

LESSON TWO
WEAPONRY

"Ninjas are masters of many weapons, like the shuriken," Raven says. She shows Beast Boy sharp stars.

"Ow!
That is pointy!
You take it,"
Beast Boy says.

LESSON THREE STEALTH

"Walk across the bubble wrap, and do not pop any!"
Robin says.

Robin shows Beast Boy how to do it
He is very good at it.

But Beast Boy thinks that popping
bubbles is way more fun.

"NOW TRAIN!" Robin says.

They work hard for a long time.

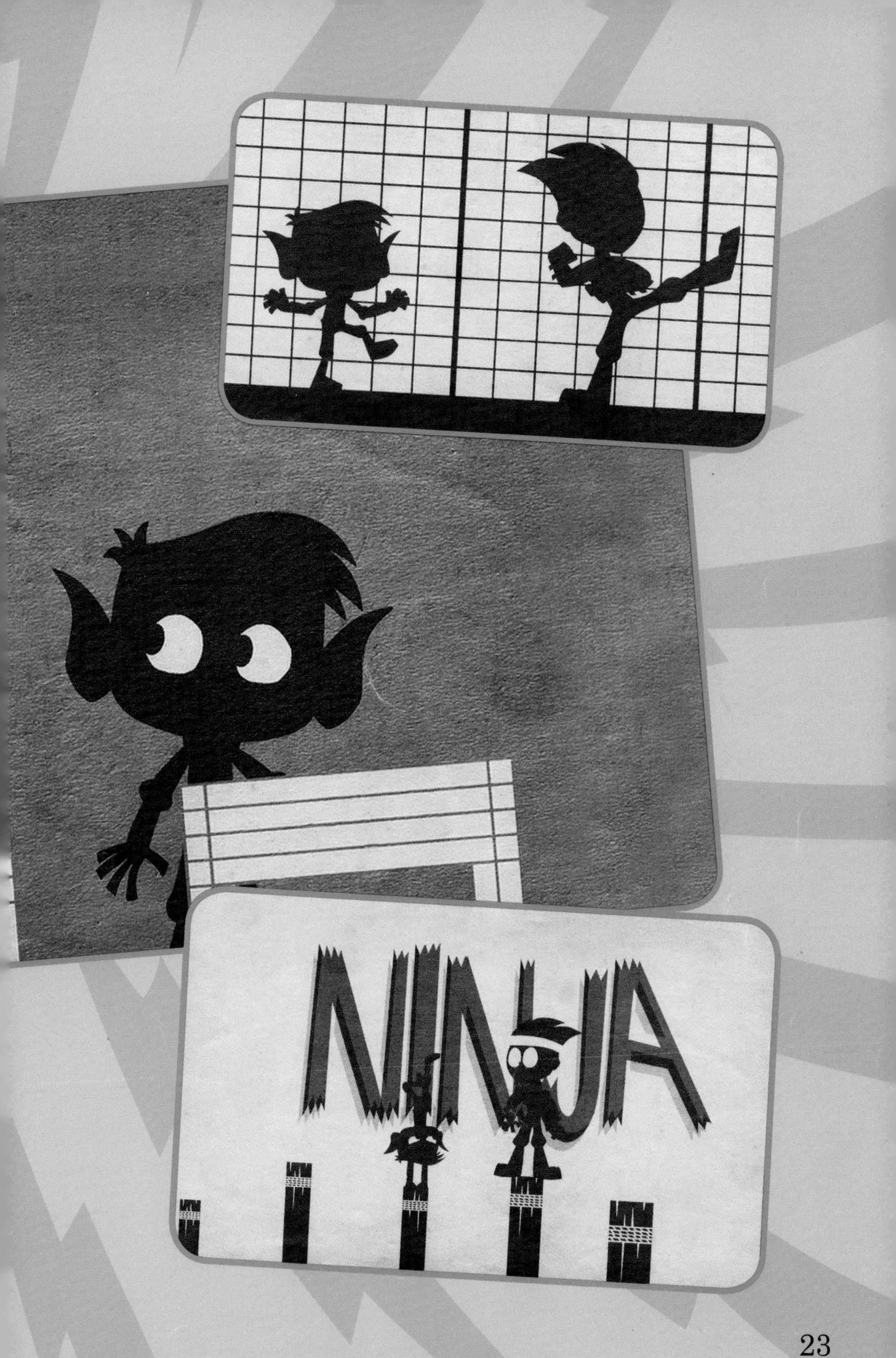
NINJA

"I am the ninja master now!"
says Beast Boy proudly.
Robin is not pleased.

"No, not yet.
You are still the student,"
Robin says.

"Oh, yeah?
Well, I am going to get
the MacGuffin first!"
Beast Boy says.

Robin loves a challenge.

"May the best ninja win!" he says.

The race is on!

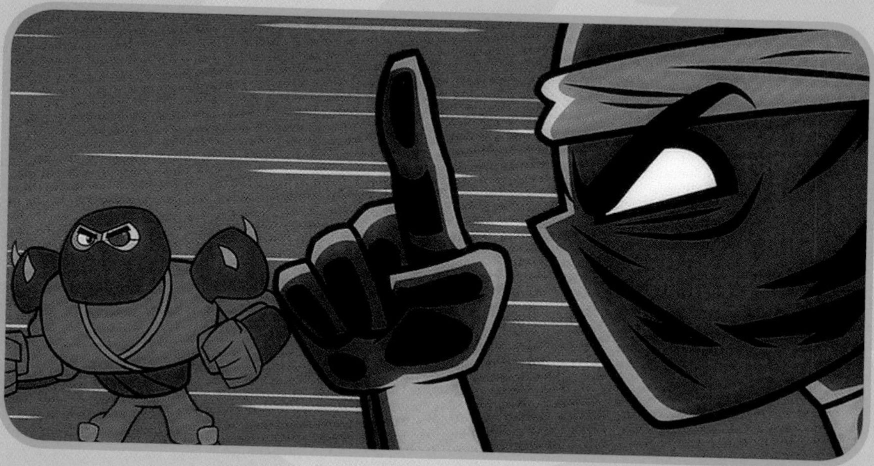

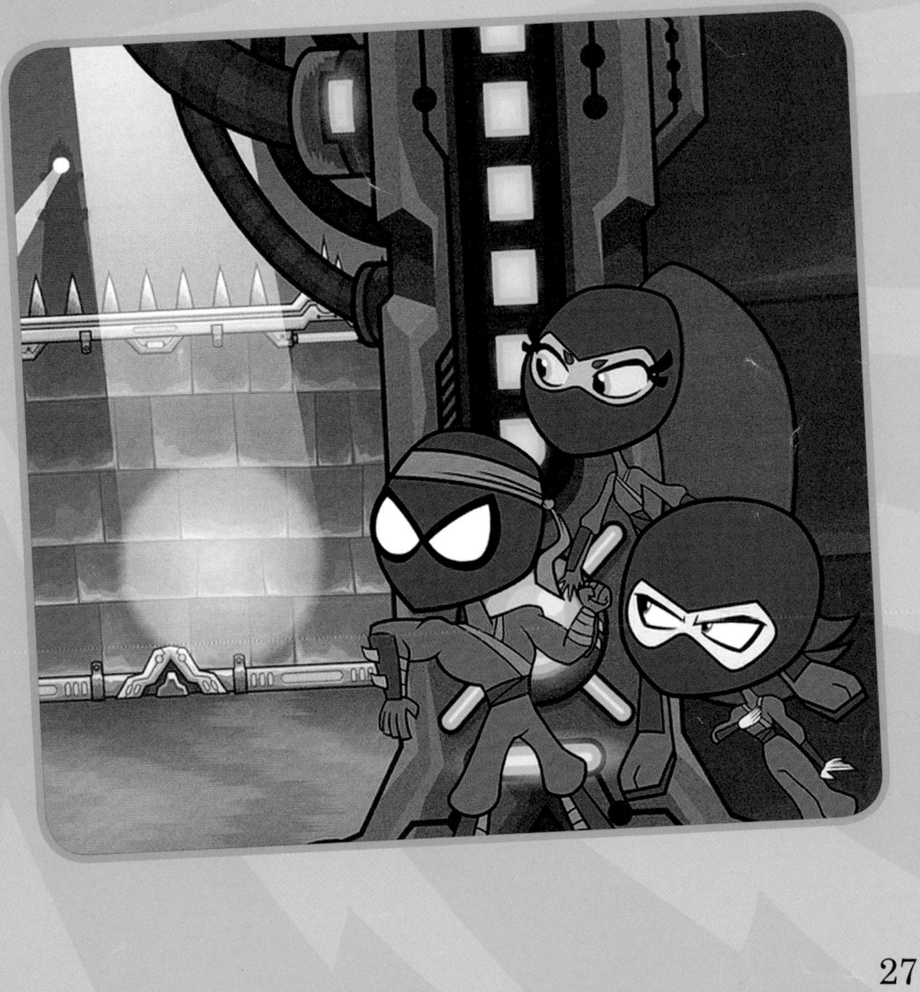

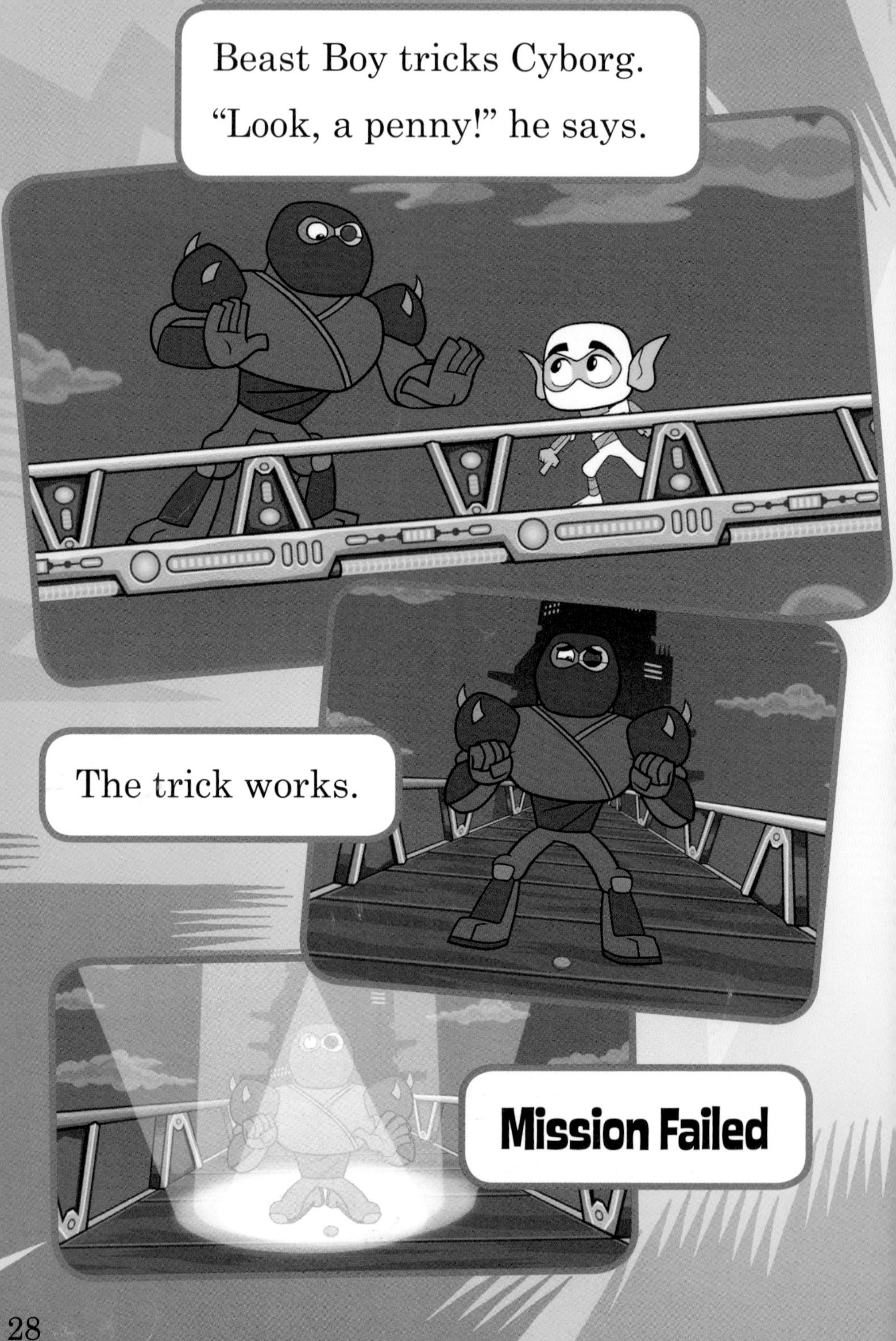
Beast Boy tricks Cyborg.
"Look, a penny!" he says.
The trick works.
Mission Failed

Starfire and Raven are not as lucky.
Beast Boy uses a gas cloud on them.

The girls are not happy.
"Ew! Silent but deadly?
Really?" Raven asks.

"Just like a ninja, yo!"
Beast Boy says.

But it is too late.

Robin reaches the MacGuffin.

He opens the special box.

He holds up his prize.

"Ha! There can only be one master," he says.

"And that is me," says Beast Boy.